THE BABY WHO WOULD NOT COME DOWN

Picture Book Studio

Joan Knight
Debrah Santini

For my brother,
Bruce Glidden MacPhail – J.K.
For Giovanni Santini – D.S.

Text copyright ©1989 Joan Knight.
Illustrations copyright ©1989 Debrah Santini.
Published by Picture Book Studio, Saxonville, MA.
Distributed in Canada by Vanwell Publishing.
All rights reserved.
Printed in Hong Kong.
10 9 8 7 6 5 4 3 2 1

Library of Congress Cataloging in Publication Data
Knight, Joan.
The baby who would not come down / Joan Knight; illustrated by Debrah Santini.
Summary: Tired of being tickled, bounced, and smothered with kisses,
a new baby floats out the window when Uncle tosses it in the air and
doesn't come down until the family mends its ways.
ISBN 0-88708-107-X
[1. Babies – Fiction.] I. Santini, Debrah, ill. II. Title.
PZ7.K738
[Bab 1989]
[E] – dc19 89-3987

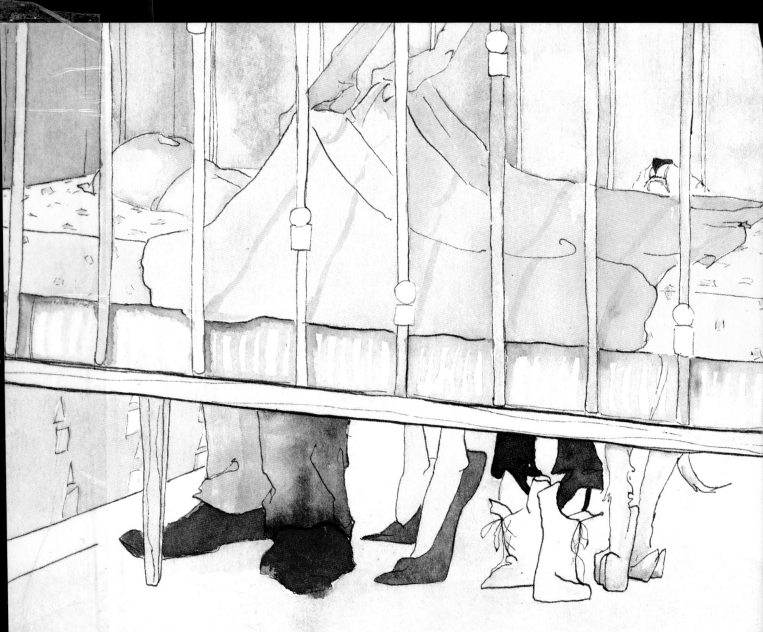

The family had a new baby. They were
pleased with the baby and the baby was
pleased with all of them, especially the dog.
But then some disturbing things happened.

Monday, the dog licked the baby and made it laugh. "Stop that!" said Mother and shooed the dog away. This made the baby sad.

Tuesday, Nurse put too many clothes on the baby so that it grew hot and sticky. The baby overheated, but Nurse did not notice. This made the baby miserable.

Wednesday, Father bounced the baby on
his knee after dinner. This made the
baby's stomach feel funny.

Thursday, the butcher tickled
the baby until it turned pink.
"See? It likes this," said the
butcher and he tickled the
baby some more. This made
the baby cross.

Friday, Sister smothered the baby with
kisses. The baby wriggled and squirmed
but Sister did not stop. This made the
baby mad.

Saturday, Uncle lit a cigar. Next he lifted
the baby out of its crib to play with it. He
tossed the baby in the air. The baby went
up and then came down. Up it went
again and down it came.

Then, an amazing thing
happened. On the third
toss, the baby did not come
down. Instead, it floated
right out the window.

No one knew what to do next.
"Come down! Come down!" they cried.
But the baby would not come down.

The family called the police. The neighbors
called the fire department.

Still, the baby hovered slightly out of reach.

That night, everybody
went to bed feeling
puzzled. They all thought
about the baby.

And that night the baby
thought about all of them.

Sunday, the family sat
down to breakfast. It
had been a rough night
but finally everybody
understood what was the
matter. The baby would
not come down because it
had had too much of some
things and not enough
of others.

And that was when the baby decided to give everybody a second chance. The family has been happy ever since…

And of course, so has the baby.